A TRAIN TO THE CITY

Annick Press gratefully acknowledges the support of the Canada Council and the Ontario Arts Council.

Canadian Cataloguing in Publication Data

Orr, Wendy
A train to the city

(Micki and Daniel ; 3)
ISBN 1-55037-282-3 (bound) ISBN 1-55037-283-1 (pbk.)

I. Ohi, Ruth. II. Title. III. Series: Orr, Wendy.
Micki and Daniel ; 3.

PS8579.R7T73 1993 jC813'.54 C92-095197-X
PZ7.077Tr 1993

The art in this book was rendered in watercolour. The text has been set in Bookman Light by Attic Typesetting.

Distributed in Canada and the USA by:
Firefly Books Ltd.
250 Sparks Avenue
Willowdale, Ontario M2H 2S4

 Printed on acid-free paper.

Printed and bound in Canada by
D.W. Friesen and Sons, Altona, Manitoba

A Train to the City

Story Wendy Orr
Art Ruth Ohi

Annick Press

M*icki Moon was skinny with straight dark hair.*

D*aniel Day was short and round with curly blond hair.*

M*icki's real name was Michelle, but she liked Micki better.*

Daniel's real name was Daniel, and that was that.

Micki Moon liked: running, jumping, shouting, singing, dancing, windy days, big waves, tall trees, horses, jumping off haystacks, climbing high rocks, being with Daniel, and fried egg and sardine sandwiches.

Daniel Day liked: playing his violin, daydreaming, playing chess, puzzles and math, calm days, floating in warm water, watching birds, lying in long grass, sleeping in haystacks, being with Micki, and fried egg and sardine sandwiches.

Micki and Daniel had been friends for as long as they could remember. When they were babies their mothers had given them pink and blue rattles and put them on a rug to play. Later they gave Micki dolls and Daniel trucks, and Micki and Daniel put the dolls in the trucks and went off and did what they liked.

Somehow, something always seemed to happen when Micki and Daniel were together . . .

Micki and Daniel had never been to the city. Their mothers often said that they would take them one day, so they could go to the zoo and the museum and the big shops and all the other things country children usually go to in the city. But somehow when the day came their mothers never really wanted to go.

Maybe it was because Daniel wouldn't go without his violin and Ooloo Mooloo and Micki wouldn't go without Pegasus.

"But parrots," said Daniel's mother, "do not go shopping."

"And round shaggy ponies," said Micki's mother, "do not visit art galleries."

But one hot summer Sunday Micki decided it was time to go.

"It's too far to walk," Daniel said.

"We don't have to walk," Micki said.

"But you won't let anyone ride Pegasus!" Daniel said, and Ooloo Mooloo nodded up and down on his shoulder.

"I don't like her to get tired," said Micki.

"Well, you can't take a horse on the train!" said Daniel.

"She's a very little horse."

"I think they'll notice," said Daniel. But he went to get his violin.

When they got to the train station Micki and Pegasus waited outside while Daniel and Ooloo Mooloo bought the tickets. The man selling the tickets was not very happy about Ooloo Mooloo.

"No pets," he said.

"He's not a pet," said Daniel. "He's a parrot."

"No animals loose on the train!" shouted the man.

"Oh, he's not loose," said Daniel. "He's on my shoulder." And Ooloo Mooloo nodded with his cheeks puffed fat.

"NO—" began the man, who was turning nearly as red as Ooloo Mooloo.

"Excuse me," said the large lady behind Daniel, "but if you don't sell me a ticket, I'll miss the train."

The man let Daniel go.

Daniel waited for the large lady and went to the gate. Micki and Pegasus stayed on the other side of the large lady.

Daniel gave the man the tickets. "My friend is just behind me," he said, and looked in the wrong direction.

The ticket man looked too. "I can't see him," he said. "But he'll miss the train if he doesn't hurry up."

The large lady gave the man her ticket.

"You can't take your dog on with you," the ticket man said to the lady.

"*What* dog?" said the lady.

"*What* dog?" said Daniel.

"*That* dog," said the ticket man, and pointed behind the lady.

"What dog?" said Ooloo Mooloo, who was sometimes a little slow to talk.

The ticket man spun around. "And you can't take a bird either!" he shouted.

Micki and Pegasus jumped on the train.

The lady said, "I'm not listening to this again," and jumped on as well.

"I have a ticket for him," Daniel said.

"But you said your friend was another boy," said the ticket man.

"No," Daniel corrected him. "*You* said my friend was another boy. But since the train's here, and there's not another boy coming, and I have two tickets, I don't suppose there's a rule that says I can't give this ticket to a parrot."

The ticket man looked confused and about ten years older than when he had started work that morning. People often looked like that when they argued with Daniel.

He pointed at the train. "Get on," he said.

Daniel took his violin and his parrot and jumped into the carriage with Micki and her pony.

"Did you get my ticket?" Micki asked.

"Not exactly," said Daniel. "But Ooloo Mooloo has one, and I don't suppose there's a rule that a parrot can't give his ticket to a girl."

More and more people came toward the carriage where Micki and Daniel, Pegasus and Ooloo Mooloo were sitting.

Micki danced back and forth from window to window. "Do you think they'll notice Pegasus?"

"Probably," said Daniel.

Micki stuck her head out the window. "I'll tell them to go away," she said.

"Wait!" shouted Daniel, "Ooloo Mooloo: baby!"

Ooloo Mooloo started to cry. He wailed and screamed and screeched and made disgusting noises like about one hundred angry babies.

All the people hurrying towards their carriage stopped and hurried even more quickly to a carriage at the other end of the train.

It was a long way to the city.

Daniel played his violin, and Micki danced a special train dance from one seat to another, and Ooloo Mooloo rocked and said "more!", and Pegasus thought. When they were tired of that they had a picnic. Micki and Daniel and Ooloo Mooloo had fried egg and sardine sandwiches, and Pegasus had her nosebag of oats.

It was quite a large nosebag for a little horse but Micki liked it much better than she had when it was a dress. Micki had been in a hurry when she made it, and quite a lot of oats always came out the other end.

Ooloo Mooloo liked that because he got oats for dessert after he had finished his fried egg and sardine sandwiches.

STATION

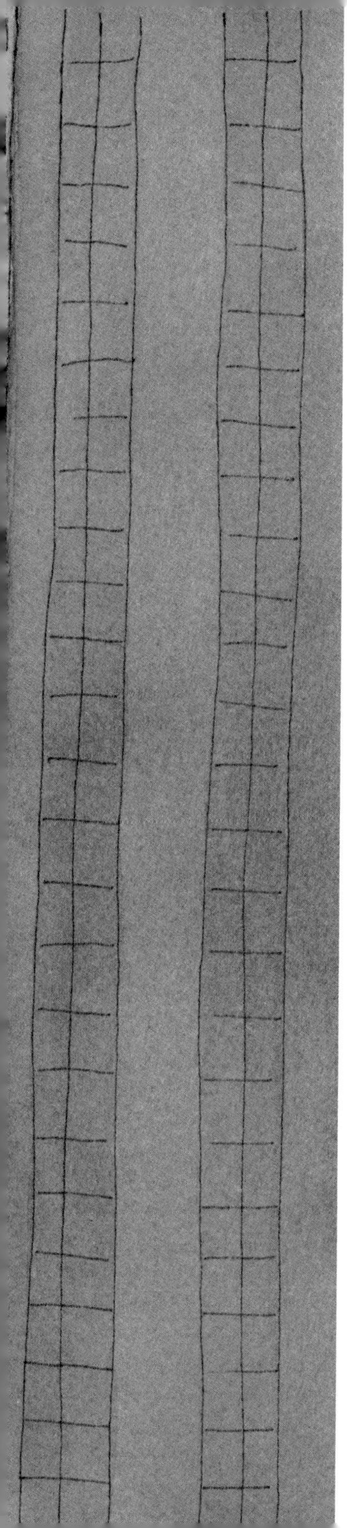

The train finally got to the city.

"How are we going to get off without anyone seeing Pegasus?" Daniel worried.

"Maybe they won't notice," Micki said.

And they didn't. Not really. The man at the gate said, "Is that a pony following you?"

And Micki and Daniel and Ooloo Mooloo said "What pony?" and the man at the gate decided that he couldn't really have seen a pony getting off a train, so he let them go.

The city was very big and very busy. Buildings and monuments and skyscrapers and shops and houses; cars and vans and buses and trucks.

"More!" said Ooloo Mooloo. "More, more, more!"

"Where should we go?" said Micki.

"A museum?" said Daniel.

"Or just walking?" said Micki.

"Maybe we could walk till we see a museum," said Daniel.

They walked and walked, up streets and down; they looked in restaurants and shop windows and they looked at old churches, at shiny tall skyscrapers and bored people's faces.

Then they saw a park. "I need a rest," said Daniel.

They flopped down on the grass between a big tall tree and a fountain. People were hurrying down the path to the other side of the park, rushing, scurrying, as if something important were going to happen there.

"I wonder where they're all going," said Micki.
"Nowhere," said Daniel. "People in the city always walk like that."
"Oh," said Micki. She had had enough sitting still. She skipped and hopped around the fountain, over the flower beds and through the trees.

Daniel started to play his violin. Soft and slow, soft and slow, then fast and wild, fast and wild, and Ooloo Mooloo started to rock and Micki started to dance, soft and slow, fast and wild, and Pegasus chewed her oats.

The people hurrying down the path to the other side of the park all stopped and hurried back. They watched while Daniel played and Micki danced and Ooloo Mooloo rocked and Pegasus chewed; then when Daniel stopped and Ooloo Mooloo shouted "More!" the people all laughed and clapped and shouted "Encore! Encore!"

So Daniel started to play again. He played and played till

he could not play any more, and Micki could not dance any more, and Ooloo Mooloo could not rock any more, and Pegasus could not eat any more.

Then the people laughed and cheered and clapped again, and said it was the best concert they had ever seen, and some of them threw flowers to Micki, and they all went away.

So Daniel packed up his violin, and Ooloo Mooloo stretched his wings and settled again on Daniel's shoulder, and Pegasus had a drink out of the fountain while Micki braided the flowers into her mane, and they followed the road at the end of the park. They bought four ice creams and ate them as they walked along. They waved to the people sitting in cars, and walked and walked until they got to another park.

“Well, it’s not exactly a park,” said Daniel.
“But there’s grass for Pegasus,” said Micki, “and a place for me to run.”
“And a place for me to sit,” said Daniel.

So Micki ran around the circle, and Pegasus went to visit some horses. Daniel had a rest, and Ooloo Mooloo said "More," but there were no more fried egg and sardine sandwiches, and Daniel was too tired to play his violin.

Micki finished running. She flopped down beside Daniel and Ooloo Mooloo. "Let's go home."

"How?" asked Daniel. "It'll take three hours and seventeen minutes to walk back to the train station. And I don't think they'll let Pegasus on again."

But Pegasus was coming back. She looked at the tall beautiful horses getting into their trailer, and she looked at Micki, and . . .

"I think Pegasus has got us a taxi," said Micki.

And she did. It took them all the way home, with Daniel playing his violin, and Ooloo Mooloo rocking and Micki dancing a special horse trailer dance—and Pegasus looking as important and pleased with herself as a round shaggy pony can look.